Exploring Our Rainforest

Red-Eyed Tree Frog

Tamra B. Orr

CHERRY
LAKE
Publishing

Published in the United States of America by Cherry Lake Publishing
Ann Arbor, Michigan
www.cherrylakepublishing.com

Content Adviser: Dr. Stephen S. Ditchkoff, Professor of Wildlife Ecology, Auburn University, Alabama
Reading Adviser: Marla Conn, ReadAbility, Inc.

Photo Credits: ©Jeff McGraw/Shutterstock Images, cover, 1, 27; ©macropixel/depositphotos, 5; ©IUCN (International Union for Conservation of Nature), Conservation International & NatureServe (2008), 6; ©Ryan Somma/http://www.flickr.com/CC-BY-SA 2.0, 7; ©Heiko Kiera/Shutterstock Images, 9, 15, 29; ©Dorling Kindersley/Thinkstock, 10; ©ABDESIGN/CanStockPhoto, 11; ©JanPietruszka/CanStockPhoto, 13; ©JanPietruszka/depositphotos, 16; ©wollertz/depositphotos, 19; ©Charles Sharp/http://www.flickr.com/CC-BY-2.0, 21; ©Brian Gratwicke/http://www.flickr.com/CC-BY-2.0, 23, 25; ©Matt Jeppson/Shutterstock Images, 26; ©worldswildlifewonders/Shutterstock Images, 28

Library of Congress Cataloging-in-Publication Data

Orr, Tamra, author.
Red-eyed tree frog / Tamra B. Orr.
    pages cm. — (Exploring our rainforests)
Summary: "Introduces facts about red-eyed tree frogs, including physical features, habitat, life cycle, food, and threats to these rainforest creatures. Photos, captions, and keywords supplement the narrative of this informational text." — Provided by publisher.
Audience: Ages 8-12.
Audience: Grades 4 to 6.
Includes bibliographical references and index.
ISBN 978-1-63188-978-3 (hardcover) — ISBN 978-1-63362-017-9 (pbk.) — ISBN 978-1-63362-056-8 (pdf) — ISBN 978-1-63362-095-7 (ebook) 1. Red-eyed treefrog—Juvenile literature. I. Title.

QL668.E24O77 2015
597.8'9—dc23   2014024967

Cherry Lake Publishing would like to acknowledge the work of
The Partnership for 21st Century Skills. Please visit www.p21.org
for more information.

Printed in the United States of America
Corporate Graphics

ABOUT THE AUTHOR

Tamra Orr is a full-time writer and author living in the gorgeous Pacific Northwest. She loves her job because she learns more about the world every single day and then turns that information into pop quizzes for her patient and tolerant children (ages 23, 21, and 18). She has written more than 350 nonfiction books for people of all ages, so she never runs out of material and is sure she'd be a champion on Jeopardy!

TABLE OF CONTENTS

— CHAPTER 1 —

Colors That Dazzle

High up in the green **canopy** of the rainforest, a snake slithers along a branch in search of a tasty snack. Its tongue darts in and out, tasting the air, in hopes of smelling a delicious tree frog. Overhead, a bat sends out its high-pitched squeak, waiting for sound waves to bounce back and help it locate a meal. A tree frog sounds perfect!

Hidden on one of the leaves is a small bump. The snake slides closer to investigate. What is it? The green bump blends in with the leaf, but there is something different about it. Suddenly, the green bump turns into a lightning-fast flash of color, something very bright and alive. The bump is now a frog, with four legs, orange toes, and blue thighs. Yellow stripes glow from its sides. And, oh, those gigantic, bulging red eyes! Startled, the snake freezes in place for a moment, giving this tiny frog the perfect chance to escape.

Red-eyed tree frogs get their name from their bulging red eyes.

RANGE MAP

ARCTIC OCEAN

Europe

Asia

North America

ATLANTIC OCEAN

PACIFIC OCEAN

Africa

PACIFIC OCEAN

INDIAN OCEAN

South America

Australia

☐ RANGE OF RED-EYED TREE FROG

Red-eyed tree frogs live in Central America.

With one push from its powerful back legs, the tree frog takes a huge leap to another leaf. It keeps jumping until it is out of danger. Whew! Once again, this rainforest creature has survived, thanks to its ability to frighten its hungry **predators**.

These frogs have extremely strong legs.

LOOK AGAIN

RED-EYED TREE FROGS ARE ABLE TO JUMP UP TO 20 TIMES THEIR OWN BODY LENGTH. IF HUMANS COULD DO THIS, THEY COULD JUMP TWO BASKETBALL COURTS IN ONE LEAP! CAN YOU THINK OF OTHER ANIMALS THAT ARE POWERFUL JUMPERS?

CHAPTER 2

UP IN THE TREES

The scientific term for red-eyed tree frogs is *Agalychnis callidryas*. The name means "beautiful tree nymphs." Wildlife organizations across the world use these little frogs as a symbol for the beauty of life in the rainforest. Once people see the frogs, with their amazing shades of color, it is almost impossible to forget them.

There are more than 600 types of tree frogs living in swampy areas of Central and South America's rainforests. They are found in Mexico, Guatemala, Belize, Honduras, Nicaragua, Costa Rica, and Panama.

As their name implies, these **amphibians** are **arboreal**. That means they spend almost all their lives in the high canopy of trees, rather than in the water or on the ground. Instead of walking or hopping, these cold-blooded creatures jump from leaf to leaf. So swift and limber, they have earned the nickname "monkey frogs."

Red-eyed tree frogs spend nearly all their time in the highest level of the rainforest, the canopy.

BODY DIAGRAM

eyes

suction
pads on
toes

These frogs' toes help them hold onto branches.

[21ST CENTURY SKILLS LIBRARY]

This frog is the right shade of green to blend in with the leaves.

When the sun is out, and much of the rainforest wildlife is starting a new day, the tree frog is preparing to go to sleep. Carefully it selects a leaf and camouflages itself by completely hiding its colors. It wants to look like nothing more than another piece of the jungle greenery. The tree frog attaches itself to the underside of the leaf and uses its sticky toes to hold on. Every morning, the frog chooses a different place to sleep. It never goes to the same spot twice.

The red-eyed tree frog uses its eyes to help keep itself safe from harm. Its three eyelids open and close from the bottom up. One eyelid has gold-colored lines running through it. This makes the eyes look almost like stained glass windows when they are closed. This special eyelid keeps items from getting in and causing damage. It is called a nictitating membrane. Dogs, birds, cats, fish, and reptiles also have three eyelids.

The red-eyed tree frog uses its eyes for one more thing—finding something to eat! It has excellent vision in the dark and uses that skill when it is time to get up and hunt.

THINK ABOUT IT

IN ORDER TO SLEEP UNDETECTED, THE RED-EYED TREE FROG HAS TO TUCK ITS FOUR LEGS TIGHTLY UNDERNEATH IT. CAN YOU THINK OF OTHER ANIMALS THAT SLEEP THIS WAY?

When they sleep, the frogs try to blend in with the leaves.

CHAPTER 3

MEAT TO EAT

At night, the red-eyed tree frog wakes up hungry. Time to find some dinner! The bottoms of its webbed feet and toes have sticky suction cups. These allow the frog to make its way along twigs and leaves without slipping or falling.

What's on the menu for the average tree frog? These frogs are **carnivores** and eat many types of insects. A fly or cricket does nicely. So do spiders or small grasshoppers. Even a smaller frog works if nothing else comes along. Right now, the hungry frog spots a moth on the next leaf and takes a giant leap. As it jumps, its long, sticky tongue shoots out, wraps around the insect, and pulls it in. Yum! It was just the right flavor.

Red-eyed tree frogs hunt for insects that also live in the canopy layer.

The jungle's rainy season helps the frogs stay healthy.

Using the suction cups on their feet, tree frogs do come down to the ground now and then. As amphibians, they have to keep their skin wet. Often they can do this by bathing in morning dew on the leaves or enjoying one of the jungle's many rain showers. That is easy to do from May to November, known as the wet season in the rainforest. From December to April, however, the dry season arrives. Puddles of water trapped on leaves and in flowers are much harder to find.

When this happens, the frogs cope in two ways. One is that their skin develops a waxy coating so it stays moist. The other way requires the frogs to crawl down the trees and find a pond, stream, or river to jump into. They soak up water through their skin.

There is another reason the frogs make their way to the ground below. When mating season rolls around, it is time to head to the water.

GO DEEPER

RED-EYED TREE FROGS ARE OFTEN KEPT IN AQUARIUMS AS PETS. WHAT WOULD THE CHALLENGES BE IN TAKING CARE OF THEM? HOW WOULD THEY BE FED?

CHAPTER 4

Mating and Laying Eggs

"Chock! Chock! Chock!" Every 10 seconds, the sound repeats.

It is the call of the male red-eyed tree frog, who is looking for a mate. To make this unusual sound, he uses a vocal **sac**. Only the male frogs have vocal sacs.

To make sure the other male frogs know to stay out of its territory, the red-eyed tree frog stands up as tall as possible on his four legs. He quivers and shakes as if having a tantrum. This behavior sends two messages. "Come and see me!" it says to the females. "Keep out!"

it warns the males. If another male tries to move in, the fight is on. The two tiny frogs wrestle until one is pinned—and becomes the loser.

When he pulls air into the sac, it looks like a balloon has expanded in his throat.

Female tree frogs come out of hiding when they hear the mating call. The females are quite a bit larger than the males, so the male jumps onto the female's back. Together, the two climb down to the nearest pond or water source. After taking water into her bladder, the female climbs onto a leaf she has chosen. It is important that the leaf hangs out over the water.

The female releases a group, or clutch, of 10 to 80 eggs on the underside of the leaf. She goes to the pond to get water and covers the eggs with it. She adds more eggs, then water, three or four more times. When the female is finally done laying eggs, the parents return to their trees, leaving the eggs to develop on their own.

Finally, the eggs tear open from all the pulling and pushing. The tadpoles tumble off the leaf into the water below. Had their parents chosen a leaf that was not over the water, the tadpoles would not have survived this process.

In most frog species, the females are bigger than the males.

LOOK AGAIN

Look at this pair of red-eyed tree frogs. How can you tell which is male and which is female?

The babies spend their days doing two things: eating and growing. They eat **algae**, as well as other plants and leaves found in the water. At first they live and breathe like fish underwater. As the weeks pass, they change. They develop back legs, then front legs. Next, they grow lungs so they will be able to breathe on land.

When the froglets crawl out of the water, they still do not look like red-eyed tree frogs. Their skin is a dull brownish-green. Their eyes are gold and brown, and they still have a tail. It will take 3 months before they develop the bright skin and huge red eyes of their parents. A year later, it will be the new generation's turn to send out the mating call.

This froglet is in between being a tadpole and an adult.

CHAPTER 5

AVOIDING PREDATORS

The pile of eggs is hidden on the underside of the leaf, waiting. About 2 weeks after they are laid, the eggs start to move. The babies inside are growing and are in motion. While they mature, they are at high risk.

Clutches of eggs are a favorite snack of many arboreal snakes. It only takes minutes for a hungry predator to munch dozens of eggs. Amazingly, red-eyed tree frog eggs can detect the vibration of an attacking predator, such as a snake or wasp. When this happens, the eggs will actually hatch early, preferring to take their chances

Female tree frogs release their eggs on leaves.

in the water instead. Scientists don't quite understand how they know to do this.

Red-eyed tree frogs are tiny, rarely growing more than a few inches long. They cannot bite or sting. They are not **toxic** like their rainforest cousins, the poison dart frogs. How do they manage to stay alive when bats,

The coral snake is one animal that eats red-eyed tree frogs.

This frog's red eyes can sometimes frighten away predators.

snakes, and other predators find them so tasty? They rely on a technique known in biology as **startle coloration**, or "flash colors." The frogs hide their bright **hues** until they feel threatened. Then they display them in of hopes of **paralyzing** their predators just long enough to make a quick getaway. First, they flash those red eyes. If that's not enough to do it, their front and back legs unfold with more color! While the predator tries to figure out what's happening, the frog escapes!

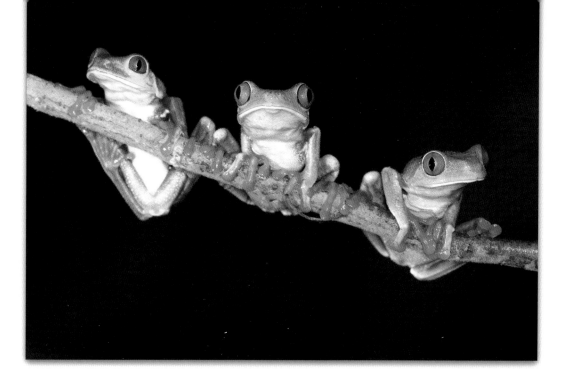

Red-eyed tree frogs are a familiar symbol of the rainforest.

Red-eyed tree frogs are not endangered. But they are threatened because rainforests are shrinking. Many environmental groups trying to save the rainforests use pictures of the red-eyed tree frog to help support their cause.

This frog is going to use its startle coloration.

LOOK AGAIN

Look closely at this photograph. Based on the colors you see, do you think this frog is feeling threatened?

THINK ABOUT IT

- In chapter 5, you learned that red-eyed tree frogs use "startle coloration" to frighten away their predators. What other animals can you think of that use this method for staying safe?

- The places where red-eyed tree frogs live are shrinking because the trees are being cut down. How might logging affect their life spans?

- Tadpoles are born with tails, but they fade away as they grow. Why do you think they have them in the first place?

- What is it about red-eyed tree frogs that has made them such a strong symbol of rainforest wildlife?

[21ST CENTURY SKILLS LIBRARY]

LEARN MORE

FURTHER READING

Abramson, Andra Serlin, and Paula Kovacs Ross. *Kids Meet the Reptiles*. Kennebunkport, ME: Applesauce Press, 2013.

Cowley, Joy. *Red-Eyed Tree Frog*. New York: Scholastic Press, 2006.

Edmonds, Devin. *Tree Frogs*. Neptune City, NJ: TFH Publications, 2012.

Netherton, John. *Red-Eyed Tree Frogs*. Minneapolis: Lerner Publications, 2001.

Phillips, Dee. *Tree Frog*. New York: Bearport Publishing, 2014.

WEB SITES

5 Cool Facts About Red-Eyed Tree Frogs
www.youtube.com/watch?v=9r8_gkHG8e0
Watch this brief video of Jungle Bob talking about these tree frogs.

National Geographic Kids—Red-Eyed Tree Frog
http://kids.nationalgeographic.com/animals/red-eyed-tree-frog.html
Read all about the red-eyed tree frog and how it survives in the rainforests.

Rainforest Animals—Red-Eyed Tree Frog
www.rainforestanimals.net/rainforestanimal/redeyedtreefrog.html
Find out which animals share the rainforest environment with the red-eyed tree frogs.

GLOSSARY

algae (AL-jee) nonflowering plant that has no stems, roots, or leaves and mainly grows in water

amphibians (am-FIB-ee-uhnz) cold-blooded vertebrates such as frogs, toads, newts, or salamanders

arboreal (ahr-BAWR-ee-uhl) living in trees

canopy (KAN-uh-pee) the cover formed by the leafy upper branches in a forest

carnivores (KAHR-nuh-vohrz) animals that eat meat to survive

hues (HYOOZ) colors, tints, or shades

paralyzing (PAR-uh-lize-eng) making something unable to move or act

predators (PRED-uh-turz) animals that hunt and eat other animals

sac (SAK) a baglike structure on an animal or plant

startle coloration (STAHR-tl kuhl-uh-RAY-shuhn) displaying colors in order to scare off a threat

toxic (TOK-sik) poisonous

INDEX